Tubby Can't Swim!

Written By:

Shirley Gould

Illustrations By:

Justin Steward

MW00893750

LifeRich Publishing is a registered trademark of The Reader's Digest Association, Inc.

LifeRich Publishing books may be ordered through booksellers or by contacting:

LifeRich Publishing
1663 Liberty Drive
Bloomington, IN 47403
www.liferichpublishing.com
844-686-9607

ISBN: 978-1-4897-3348-1 (sc)
ISBN: 978-1-4897-3349-8 (e)

Print information available on the last page.

LifeRich Publishing rev. date: 04/24/2021

This book is dedicated to my amazing grandchildren

Madi, Jake, Finley, Charlotte, Judah, Blakely, & Lyda

You keep a smile on my face…love you ShoSho

"Good morning Safariland!"

Gabby, the African Grey parrot welcomed the day.

"Wake up animals. It's time to play!"

She flapped her wings and stretched her neck.

Bobby, the baby baboon, looked over a log.

Molly, the mongoose, stood and yawned. **"Morning Gabby."**

"Hello, Molly." Gabby flew over her head. "It's going to be a fine day."

Tubby was waiting by Gabby's favorite tree.

"Hi, Gabby."

Tubby, the baby hippo hung his head.

"My Mama is still eating.
I came to talk to you."

Gabby flew down to the ground.

"What's wrong, Tubby? You look sad."

"I am sad. Hippos stay in the water all day. But I can't swim."

The fish stuck her head out of the water, wiping moisture off her face with her fin.

"What's up, Gabby?"

Can you tell him how to swim?"
Gabby asked.

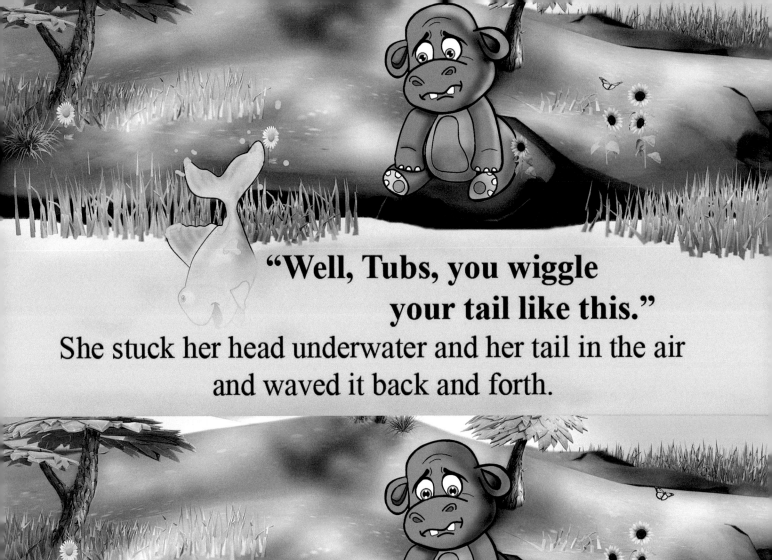

**"Well, Tubs, you wiggle
your tail like this."**
She stuck her head underwater and her tail in the air
and waved it back and forth.

**"Then you flap your
fins like this."**
Finley showed him how.

"But I don't have fins or a tail like yours." Tubby said as a tear fell from his eye.

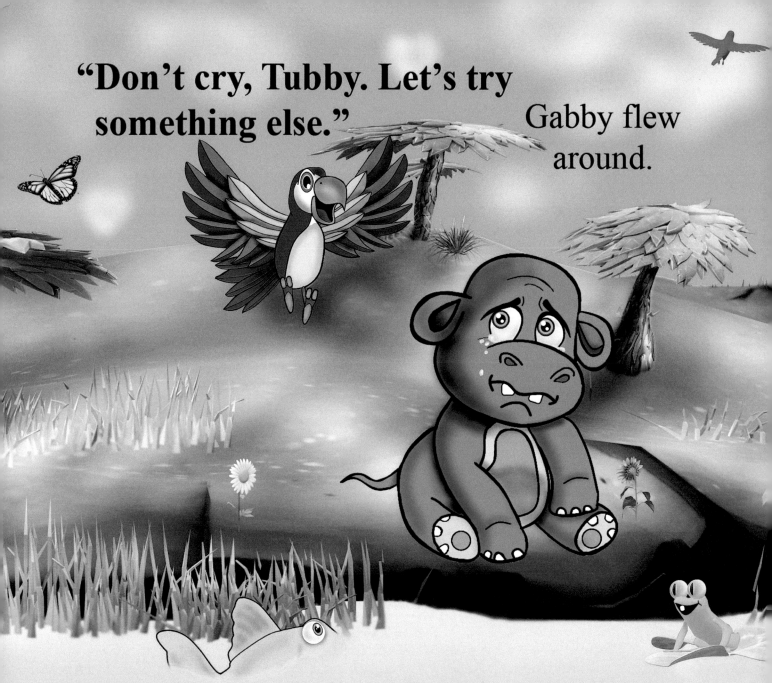

"Don't cry, Tubby. Let's try something else." Gabby flew around.

"Ducks can swim. Caesar and Delilah, where are you?" Gabby Squawked.

Two Egyptian geese swam that direction.
"Quack, quack. What's happening, Gabby?"

"Tubby is sad. He can't swim."
Gabby landed on Tubby's back.
"Please help him."

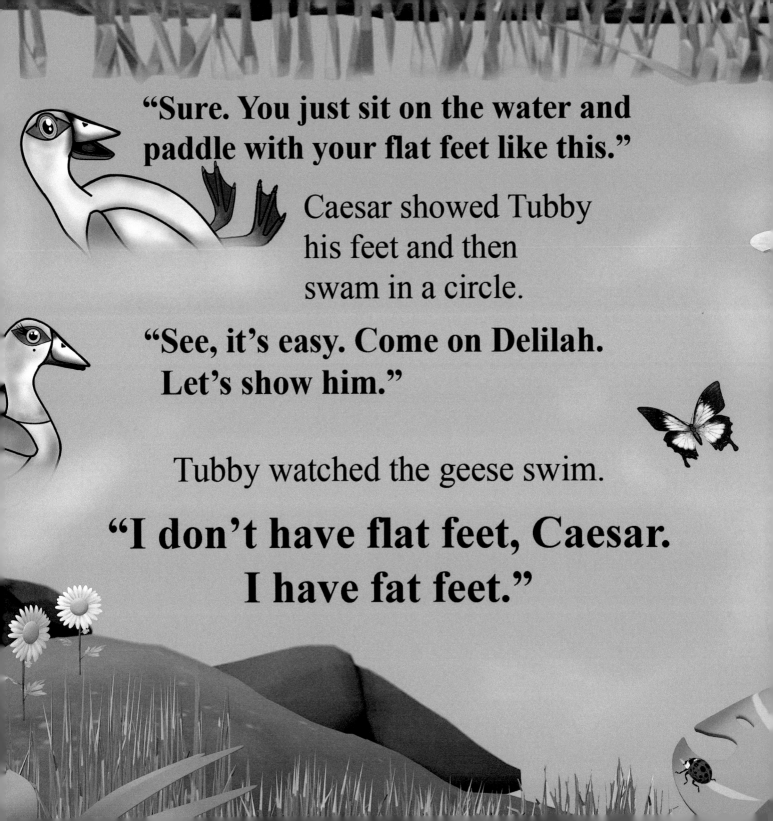

"Sure. You just sit on the water and paddle with your flat feet like this."

Caesar showed Tubby his feet and then swam in a circle.

"See, it's easy. Come on Delilah. Let's show him."

Tubby watched the geese swim.

"I don't have flat feet, Caesar. I have fat feet."

"Oh, I see. Maybe Crockett, the crocodile could help you. He swims."
Caesar and Delilah swam down river.

Crockett looked at Tubby.
"Okay. Just Push off into the water with your four little feet and move your big tail from side to side and you'll be swimming."

"But, Crockett, I have four big feet
and my tail is short and small."

"It's hopeless.
I'll never learn to swim."

He shook his head.

He started to cry.

Gabby flew by and wiped his tears.
"Don't cry Tubby. It will be okay somehow."
She perched in the tree.
"Tubby, I see your mother
coming this direction."

"She will be ready to go into the river.
What do I do?"

Mrs. Hooty, the wise old owl,
flew to the big acacia tree.
**"Morning Mrs. Hooty." Gabby said.
"Tubby has a big problem."**

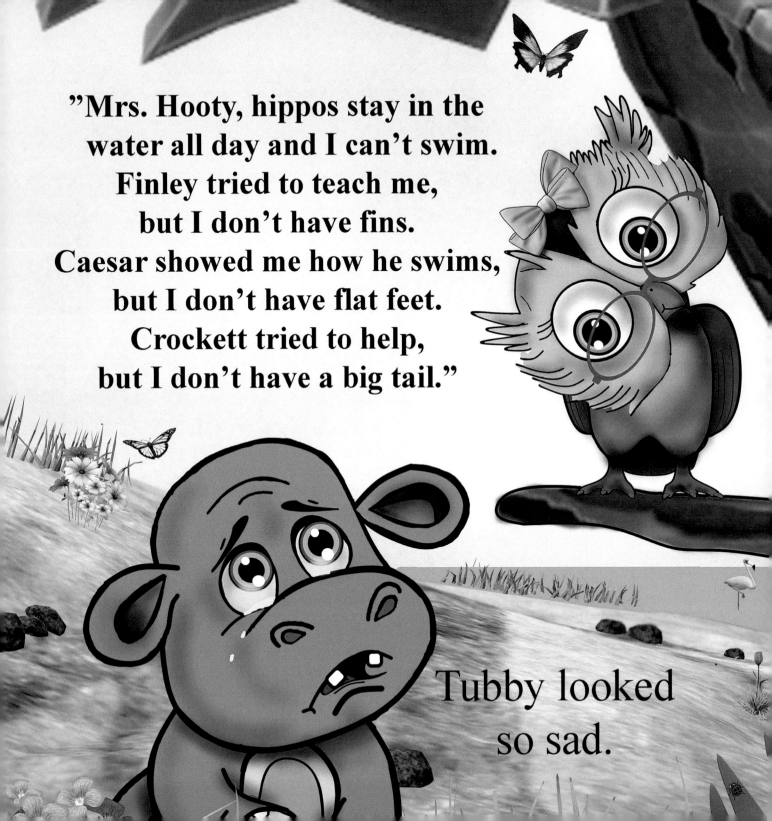

"Mrs. Hooty, hippos stay in the water all day and I can't swim. Finley tried to teach me, but I don't have fins. Caesar showed me how he swims, but I don't have flat feet. Crockett tried to help, but I don't have a big tail."

Tubby looked so sad.

"Hoot, hoot, who you?"
What's the matter, Tubby?"
The old owl leaned forward
and tilted her head.

Mrs. Hooty stood straighter on her perch.

"Tubby, hippos can't swim.
They move their front legs like the wild dogs do,
but they're too heavy to propel their bodies
through the water.
Hippos stay in shallow water and push off
the muddy bottom, get air and then dive
under again."

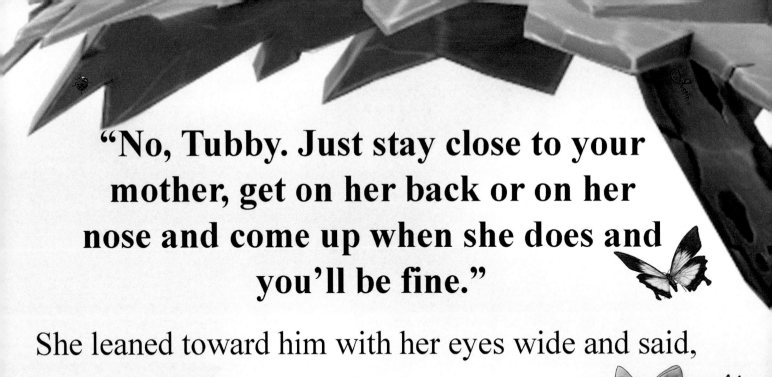

"No, Tubby. Just stay close to your mother, get on her back or on her nose and come up when she does and you'll be fine."

She leaned toward him with her eyes wide and said,

"You're a hippo. Act like a hippo, not a fish, not a goose, or a crocodile. Be the best hippo you can be."

"Thanks, Mrs. Hooty. You are so smart." Tubby smiled.

"Mrs. Hooty is smart.
She's a wise old owl."
Gabby sang as she flapped her wings.

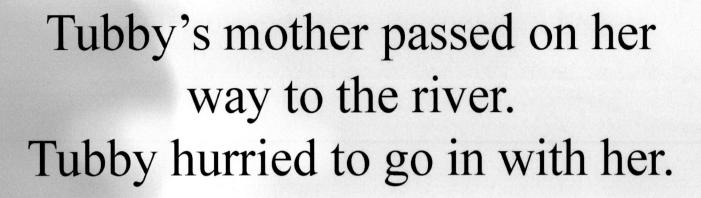

Tubby's mother passed on her
way to the river.
Tubby hurried to go in with her.

Splash,
  splash.

They waded in and
disappeared under water.

Before long the mother hippo came up for air
with tubby on her back.
Tubby smiled really big, his teeth shining.

"He's a happy hippo now." Gabby flew in a circle.

"Tubby is happy and I'm glad. **It's a great day in Safariland!**"

"A great day indeed!" Bobby, the bashful, baby baboon shouted.